Little Bird Stories

Volume Nine

Selected by Cherie Dimaline

Invisible Publishing
Halifax & Picton

Cataloguing data available from Library and Archives Canada

Cover and interior design by Megan Fildes | Typeset in Laurentian
With thanks to type designer Rod McDonald

Printed and bound in Canada

Invisible Publishing | Halifax & Picton
www.invisiblepublishing.com

We acknowledge the support of the Canada Council for the Arts and the Ontario Arts Council.

Canada Council   Conseil des Arts
for the Arts   du Canada

ONTARIO ARTS COUNCIL
CONSEIL DES ARTS DE L'ONTARIO
an Ontario government agency
un organisme du gouvernement de l'Ontario

Little Bird Stories

Volume Nine

Selected by Cherie Dimaline

ABOUT THE CONTEST

I LOVE TO WATCH TIME-LAPSE VIDEOS OF ARTISTS AT WORK. A hand-lettered sign magically forming in a window, a lush seascape blooming in watercolour, fondant flowers growing petal by petal over the top of a cake. I watch time-lapse videos of leaves sprouting from tree branches for the same reason—it's utterly fascinating to watch something form out of nothing.

It's harder to see the writing process. Our work isn't pretty to watch in its becoming. And if we write on a computer, our process isn't even visible.

Write a story that starts with an ending. Give your character an unusual watch, use the words "striped" and "innovative" somewhere, and end your story with fruit.

Knowing the writing prompt these writers used is a way we get to see traces of their imagination at work.

When you find these clues embedded in these three stories, you may feel a little thrill: look! Here's the way a writer makes something out of nothing!

Each writer used the prompt differently; each used these random words and imbued them with special power for their own story.

Knowing this part of their process can make it feel like you have access to a secret door as you read. It feels like you can see a piece of their creative impulse.

But of course, it's still a mystery.

Stories need character, yearning, emotion, presence, time, and an unsolvable problem, just for starters. None of that can be found in a writing prompt.

Where do ideas come from?

Maybe the answer has something to do with our desire to make meaning and to share our human experience with each other. And for the thrill of making something from nothing.

I hope you enjoy reading this year's winning Little Bird stories. If you like them, please share this book with someone when you are finished.

Sarah Selecky

PREFACE

I RECENTLY ATTENDED A FESTIVAL IN MONTREAL where two-time Governor General Award-winning author and Order of Canada recipient Tim Wynne-Jones told us that story allows us to grow in empathy and to become more human. So then this is the role of the writer—*to make people more human*. What a heavy, gorgeous responsibility.

I love short stories. Done with skill, they are perfectly molded, expertly crafted portraits of a time or a place or a personality. They are framed by structure and theme, coloured in with cadence and character, and hung with authorial voice. Short stories can be curated by writers and readers alike, arranged in such a way that they map out a way through, ordered so that we know where to step, or where to not step.

This year's Little Bird Contest delivered a gallery of perfectly molded, expertly crafted stories. I spent weeks walking down illuminated hallways, turning around in rooms filled to burst, taking in the described lush backyards, slow smiles and desperate actions that reminded why I read, and even more so, why I write.

In "The Catherine Series," we are confronted with the turmoil of complacency and the satisfying ache of the search. This story is a scream in a closed room, a sprint to live in every cell while you're sitting perfectly still. I am in awe of the connective power of each word and the ways in which they were wielded.

"Father King" is hilarious as only truly tragic stories can be. I read this once through fast—not able to slow down or pause for breath because of the cadence and tension. After, I went back and savoured each line to appreciate the magnificent craft work that brought it all together.

"The Party Porch" brought me fully into my own physical body and at the same time, pulled me completely into the landscape and minds of the characters. I burned and raged, became vulnerable and gained strength, all in the span of these few pages. And all the while, marveled at the sheer beauty of the writing.

Every submission this year was a spell, a stroke of textual magic arcing out over what can sometimes be a bleak world. I was entertained, built-up, and torn back down only to be assembled once more. These writers are true magicians.

And each of these selected stories accomplished the writer's mission as laid out by Wynne-Jones. Each one of them creating empathy, and each one making us just a little bit more human. I am so grateful to share this writing life with every one of you.

Cherie Dimaline

THE PARTY PORCH
REA TARVYDAS

LIQUOR POOLED IN THEIR GUTS *and liquor burned while she slept, liquor broke down the porch door and split the crotch of her jeans, and she slumped from her life as a good girl into her new life as a slut, to stares at her naked body, her naked body, dragged across floorboards with a burning between her bruised thighs. Passed out on a party porch and they forced her face into a striped pillow, and now her blue eyes are black.*

I'm out of lipstick and, like any teenage girl with any self-respect, I steal it from the drugstore. Under the watchful eye of the pharmacist I edge past the magazine rack, read the shampoo labels before arriving at the heaven that is drugstore makeup.

They're out of my regular "Reckless Red" and I'm forced into pinks, never a good choice for a redhead. Red lipstick, plaid shirt, Vans. That's my look, my best "put together" look, no matter the season. But there's no "Reckless Red" and I'm out of my comfort zone. I'm sampling pinks. Lines of lipstick on my forearm, pink razors.

Ditch the pinks and rummage on the lowest shelf for the

theatrical make-up: purple, grey, puce, black. "Innovative Black" says the label. I add a thick line of black to my pink, razor line stamp.

Knock a couple rows of mascaras and eyeliners onto the linoleum floor, crouch down and slip the black lipstick into my tube sock. Clear up the remainder of the make-up strewn across the aisle like pick-up sticks, return them to their crooked hangers.

Done and dusted.

Curious, I lick my striped forearm just to see what old drugstore lipstick samples taste like: dust, used cooking oil, and desperation.

"What are you doing?" The clerk rounds the corner in her clunky nurses' shoes, brushes the rotating rack, whizzes the pulp paperbacks into a high-speed spin. She squeaks to a halt in front of me. Louis L'Amour chases Stephen King chases romance novels with big-breasted idiots swooning in the arms of a pirate—the spinning rack of hell.

"I dropped a couple things." I hold the mascara out like a peace offering.

"Let me put that on the front counter for you, young lady." The clerk grabs the mascara and marches over to the cash register. She pirouettes, and purses her fleshy lips into a fake smile in my direction. Orange lipstick, probably Avon. From those stupid parties the moms all go to, attendance taken like homeroom period, because surviving small-town life means mandatory attendance at Avon parties.

I have got to get out of this town.

When I pick up Wanda, we drive around town, passing the time. I gun it down Main Street a couple of times, skid around the corners, just to see what everyone is doing, if anyone is making a move to the party. Nothing.

Up ahead, a figure crouches on top of the green mailboxes. It's the new kid, Andy, and he's talking to himself again. He's wearing a porkpie hat pushed back on his head, casual, and black skinnies.

Swerving into the ditch, I pump the brakes and roll up alongside the mailboxes, but the hatchback sputters into a stall. "Uh, Andy?"

"Watcha, Marty-bird." Andy stands at attention and salutes.

"What a fucking weirdo," says Wanda from the passenger's seat.

"His mom told my mom she's worried about him. Says moving from London, England, is really hard," I say in a loud voice so Andy can hear me, because he needs to get his shit together.

"What's so hard about this town?" asks Wanda. I ignore her. She's snotty lately, ever since she got together with Al, which she won't admit to me, under no circumstances. As if I don't know about her and Al making out at the river party a couple of weeks ago. As if I haven't reminded her that Al is a complete asshole.

"There's a party tonight, Andy," I say.

"Where's that at, eh?" asks Andy and I give him detailed directions. This is a game we go through each weekend, the one where I tell him where the party is and he doesn't show up. But he needs to know the exact location, just in case.

Andy salutes again and pulls a transistor radio from the back pocket, flicks it on and holds it close to his ear.

"What're you listening to?" asks Wanda but I know she doesn't care. She doesn't care about anything these days except Al. She's obsessed with him. Probably writes lists in her journal about the details of their wedding reception at the Catholic Hall. As if Al isn't a complete asshole.

"Top of the Pops." Andy laughs too high, too loud.

"Andy, in Canada you bring your own beer to the party," I say.

"Right. Catch you later, Marty-bird," says Andy.

Shrugging, I drift into first gear and the hatchback rolls away down Riverside Road until the engine catches, rough. We buzz out onto the TransCanada and back along Solsqua Road. At the bridge, the Eagle River is low, circling lazily in the heat of a dying summer.

➻➺

At the party Wanda spots Al parking his truck in the turn-around, and takes off. I stumble down steep steps. The old house is perched on stilts high up on CPR Hill. Music rattles the old, single pane windows, Cheap Trick at Budokan by the sounds of it, and there's the crashing sound of trains coupling in the rail yard below.

On the back deck, a group of guys smoking pot guards the door. Levis and long hair. There's Mike and Sid and

Kev, and all the rest of their friends from high school and the hockey team. Their circle is shapeless, unknowable, but the outside light is on and casts strange shadows.

"Black lips. Niiiiiiice," says Sid. His eyes are mean.

"Fuck you, Sid," I reply in a cool voice and slide past the guys.

"Reading any more of those weird books, Marty?" Sid's hand shoots out and grabs my elbow, hard, too hard. He's always been a grabber, even in kindergarten.

"*Catcher in the Rye* is literature, you idiot." I twist out of his gross, grabby hands, almost losing my balance.

"Leave her alone, Sid," says Mike and Sid punches him.

The house is bursting, full of teens drinking and laughing and staring at one another, strangers in Budokan, whatever that is, wherever that is. Korea? A game of beer pong stretches down the dining room table, anchored at either end by waves of empty bottles. I stash my beer behind the sofa and search for a place to stand that's out of the way.

In an unexpected move, Andy shows up carrying tall cans of British lager in a brown paper bag. We stand together in the hallway sipping warm beer and listening to the music. When it's time Andy flips the album over on the turntable and cranks up the volume.

Side B starts with a riveting drum solo and it's impossible not to move, even the stoners are dancing. "Wicked, wicked beats," says Andy and breaks into a knee-shredding, air guitar solo. "Ain't that a Shame," shout-sings the living room crowd in unison.

Wanda finally shows up, holding hands with Al, and they head right to the kitchen. We follow her. There are a couple forty-ounce bottles of rye and vodka on the counter, god knows who brought them. Al pours Wanda a big glass of CC, and she chases it with a small amount of warm, flat Coke.

"Take it easy, Wanda," I say and she ignores me.

Al gives me a dirty look and steers Wanda into the living room.

"What a complete wanker," says Andy and pulls out an old-fashioned pocket watch clipped onto a gold chain. I've never seen one before.

"Why are you carrying that?"

Andy looks surprised. "My granddad gave it to me."

It isn't long before Wanda is spectacularly drunk and spins around in the living room, gives me the finger from three hundred and sixty dizzying degrees and falls down onto the rag rug.

I haul her up by the armpits. In her ear, mid-hoist, I say, "Wanda, don't do that. Don't."

"You're a loser. All the guys say so. A redheaded loser with black lipstick. That's what Al says and he's right," says Wanda, shaking her head, a drunk flush high on her cheekbones.

"Wanda, he's not a nice guy." I grip her by the upper arms and give her a little shake.

"Don't ruin this for me, Marty."

She pulls away and disappears into the front porch with Al.

Andy says, "You all right, Marty-bird?"

I shake my head. I need to be alone.

The house is throbbing and outside, the stairs up to the street are at a standstill. A traffic jam. I tell the guy standing one rung ahead of me that I'm going to puke and that clears a path, right quick.

It's dark by then, an indigo-blue, and the stars are out, the fucking stars, so beautiful that I can't believe they're real. And I realize the main reason I came to the party is to drive away, to drive the long way out to the Welcome Inn, in the indigo-blue dark.

⸺

"You want coffee, hon?" asks the waitress who, far as I can tell, always works graveyards. I can't remember her first name but she's definitely a Svoboda. The Svoboda family is big enough to form their own softball team, but I've never been able to tell them apart.

Slide the gingham curtain aside for a better view of the parking lot. No one. The secondary road out front of the Welcome Inn is brimming with big rigs, idling, waiting for their lucky drivers to reclaim them for their journeys out of town. Orange running lights glow in the indigo-blue dark like beacons.

The Welcome Inn is long and narrow, one line of tables parked beneath one line of windows, and a long Formica counter that no one sits at unless they have to. At one end is a separate dining room for the truckers, tucked behind squeaky saloon doors.

The front door of the diner crashes open.

Mike stumbles across the metal grate. He's stinking drunk and laughing too high, too loud. He wanders up to the counter and takes a seat on a Naugahyde stool, right in front of the pie case.

"Cherry pie. The whole fucking thing."

"Don't you swear at me, Mike Kostash." The waitress

puts her chapped hands on her skinny hips.

"Aw, c'mon. Cherry pie is the fucking best."

The waitress disappears into the kitchen.

Mike groans and holds his head in his hands. He stares at the pie case. The floating glass case is bolted to the wall and consists of two glass shelves and a sliding glass door. There's a tilted mirror in the back so you can see the pies from another angle. It holds three pies and the type varies, but there's always a lemon meringue, liquid sugar tears beading.

I pour cream into my coffee and try not to think about the lemon meringue, too many calories. My jeans are too tight. I mentally prepare myself for whatever happens next because it always happens when Mike is fucked up.

It isn't long before Mike scoots around the end of the counter and slides open the pie case. He's got the cherry pie in both hands by the time the waitress emerges from the kitchen with the fry cook, a burly guy, mid-thirties, with old acne-scars on his cheeks and tattoos on his arms.

"Mike, you ought to be ashamed of yourself," calls the waitress.

The fry cook nods once, flexes his hands into fists and glances down at his tattooed forearm. It's old, black ink and the lines are blurry. I don't know where he comes from, but I'm thinking prison.

"Cherry pie is the fucking best." Mike is swaying.

"You're paying for the whole pie," says the waitress. Mike says something about not paying for it, about not having enough money in his wallet.

"Yes, you're paying. Gimme your keys," says the fry cook and slowly cracks his knuckles, one hand at a time. Silence.

Mike winds up and chucks his keys across the counter at him. The fry cook catches them, disappears into the kitchen.

"Do you want me to call your mother, Mike?" The waitress points at the rotary dial phone hanging on the wall behind the cash register.

"My mother? The widow?" Mike laughs hysterically, his cheeks flushing. His eyes fill with tears and I know it's on account of his dad dying last year. Then he ricochets across the aisle to the empty table and slams the tin plate down. After he takes a seat, he breaks the pie into pieces with his bare hands and starts eating. And when he's had enough, he dabs and smears cherry guts on the worn tabletop. That's when he starts crying, rubs his stained hands on the thighs of his jeans, over and over again.

When he catches me staring, he says, "I didn't do anything, Marty."

"You didn't do anything, what?"

"I didn't do anything. They put me in there with her."

"With who?"

"Wanda."

"Mike, who put you in there? Who—"

"The guys. Al and Sid and—"

I grab my purse and fish out a two-dollar bill, fling it at the pale, graveyard-shift Svoboda waitress as I sprint past. My Vans squeak on the gritty linoleum floor. I drive as fast as I can to the old house on CPR Hill.

>-<

With Andy's help, I haul Wanda out of the front porch and up the stairs and lay her on the grass by the side of the road. No clothes, she's got no clothes on. I wrap her in a blanket from the back of my car. We haul her into the hatchback, drive her home and leave her, covered up, in the front yard of her folks' house, and she's got no clothes on. I ring the bell and run.

I have got to get out of this town.

Sour plums. Sour plums in the yard. She had to pick them all. It was canning season and Mom said they had to put them up, no excuses. Peaches, plums, apricots. It was never-ending.

The kitchen was full of steam, pans of hot water bubbling, and a gritty film of sugar syrup over everything, and she was at the table, pitting fruit. Dropping it into the lemon-water bowl.

"Where's my extra paring knife?" asked Mom and fumbled through the junk drawer.

"I don't know," she said. She had sharpened the old knife and hid it under her mattress, for safekeeping. Late at night she scraped the skin off the bruises, the busted fruit on her thighs. Nicks and crosses that turned red, redder, red, redder. I am what I have done. What have I done?

THE CATHERINE SERIES
ANNA RUMIN

I FOUND THE NEST QUITE BY MISTAKE—had I not been pulling out weeds I would never have seen the four eggs peeking out from the branches of the stunted pine. Thinking back, I hadn't been paying attention to the racket outside my bedroom window—the clacking of her bill, her trilling, flapping, fluttering wings as she soared from branch to branch in her attempt to protect the unborn babies. So much noise for such a small creature. Even then I thought, *she built it too low—what was she thinking?*

When the girls came home I showed them what I had found and they promised to help keep Oliver away from the tree. We didn't mention the raccoons that prowled at night or the owls we heard as we lay in bed. And we didn't anticipate who else, what else was watching the eggs.

In those days everyone used to tell me how lucky I was having *two whole months in the country* and I would smile, shrug my shoulders and agree because, really, what else could I say? Jeff was in the city and would drive up some weekends, and I felt lucky to have the time to paint while the kids swam, hiked, and played at day-camp. I was surrounded by mountains with names like Sleeping Bear, Hawk's Head, and Devil's Glen, golden fields of wheat and corn, and from my porch a path made three generations earlier by my grandmother leading to the lake, to our dock, where I would sit and paint. My paintings of the local farmer's market were popular and sold well—the more I painted, the more they wanted and not only the tourists, but the locals who told me I could capture a moment on a canvas; a child biting into ripe cherry tomatoes, a bearded blue-grass quartet, the indigo-blue pottery stand. As I write this I can only think how perfect those months were. It might have been a cliché, and I was ungrateful.

I happened to be in the gallery when Henry walked in. "Henry short for Henrietta" she said as she held out her hand and congratulated me on my new collection. "Your apple orchard series—it's paradise with a hint of naughti-ness." She bought a triptych—a child with a bucket sur-rounded by fallen apples, the child and an apple, and a close up of fallen apples all set against a blushing sky. She looked familiar I said, had we met perhaps? It turned out that yes, we had met last November at a museum gala in the city. I remembered her because she was wearing her great-grandmother's royal blue gown, her mass of auburn hair piled on her head like a nest, and she had managed to get up on a table and dance until she was taken down by security. We had a good laugh and I invited her for dinner.

"Thank you," she said. "I would love to—and I know where you live because I have boated by while you are painting and watched you."

How astonishing, I later thought, to admit to spying and naturally I was flattered, although my daughter later told me that this was creepy. *Sketchy* was the word she used. I bought sausages and corn and soon after the girls got home, Henry arrived.

It was a fun night—Henry had lived for years in Nairobi and told tales of the Kenyan bush—the lions and cubs she had watched from a truck, the giraffes who crooned and leaned into her hand when she offered them food, the elephant mothers who pushed their calves out of mud—in fact, Henry said, "there is no mammal superior to the elephant matriarch." My children sat and listened and begged for more stories and she obliged them. The lone male elephant who charged her, the goat she bought at market and slaughtered, butchered, and cooked over an open fire in the evening, the snakes she avoided when hiking along the river's edge. Later, I found an old bottle of Amarula left behind by some cottage guest, which thrilled Henry, who raised her glass to the elephants who first ate and got drunk on the fruit from the Marula tree. It was so sweet, so smooth.

It must have been a few days after that dinner when my youngest ran into the kitchen saying the eggs had hatched and did she have to go to camp—could she not stay and watch? Her older sister convinced her that watching would only unnerve the mother, and so they left with the promise that they would race back at the lunch break and look into the nest. Her older sister had also developed a crush on one of the boys at camp. I knew this because she had told me so, in secret of course.

I had completed a set of sketches the day before and was ready to begin a new series of paintings. I had never painted wildlife before but the nest, the eggs, the cautious but careless mother had called to me. So, I had found myself sitting in front of the nest and sketching the eggs, the leaves that shaded them, playing with my water-colours finding hues and tones to show the strength and fragility of the eggs and nest. I examined photographs of birds and used those to sketch what I thought the mother looked like. I listened to her wine, rasp and chirp angrily and so I moved my chair further away.

"Where is the father?" my youngest had asked and I wasn't sure so I said *the mother was a widow, the father has died, has been eaten, or maybe* but I didn't want to say *he left* and I left it at that.

So, we named the mother Catherine and to pay tribute to her new life, I was creating the Catherine Series. Jeff called in the evenings and the girls would fill him in on their lives at camp, their sailing progress, tennis medals won or not, but mostly they spoke about Catherine and her babies, and how they had just hatched and couldn't he please come down, they hadn't seen him in weeks, and didn't he want to see the babies? He was working on an *innovative project*, so no he couldn't, but he would in a few weeks and he would stay right until the end of the summer—a whole week.

I was largely absent for these conversations, and feigned the girls' need for privacy with their dad while I sat out on the porch, or gardened, or retreated to my paints. I still wasn't sure what to say to the girls, if anything at all. I still wasn't sure what I thought, what I felt, what I would do. We were going through a shitty time and the summer was a convenient if not necessary break.

It was just before lunch when Henry called out from her kayak. I was due for a break and the girls were coming home soon, so I got up and met her in the kitchen. I remember now her round sunglasses and the hair, all her dark auburn hair that covered her shoulders and back, and I remember trembling when I saw her wrist. Her wrist of all things and not that she was wearing bangles or bracelets or a watch. Her wrist was bare and thin and I could see the blue veins at her palm. I can't remember now whether it was when I was taking the bread out of the bag or cutting the cheese or when I got up and bumped into her, yes it was then, it must have been, that she kissed me and I kissed her back. And then the door opened and the girls rushed in, and together, the four of us slipped out to peer into the nest. Four tiny heads, barely heads really, the hint of heads with eyes still closed waiting to welcome the world. I'm not sure how long we watched—all I remember is Henry leaning on my back.

I managed to paint five paintings of the Catherine Series in the next five days. "It's a story," my eldest said, and indeed each painting told a piece of the story of Catherine becoming a mother: her nest in the stunted pine, the eggs, the perfect little heads, the little eyes—now open and waiting.

And every day I waited for Henry to arrive. And every day she did, just before dinner. She would arrive armed with treats—spanakopita, curried shrimp, and chapati that she said she made herself. And every night we would play games. One night we had to say what animal we would be in our next life. Henry listened and offered analysis. My eldest wanted to be lion, and so she was brave, courageous, willing to fight for what she believed in; my youngest wanted to be a dog, and so she was faithful, loyal and committed, and I hesitated between the elephant ma-triarch and a bird. Just like our Catherine!

"Ah," said Henry "of course. Birds are the bridge be-tween spirits and humans, they enjoy freedom whereas the elephant is wise and grounded and understands limi-tations." We didn't question her analysis, we soaked it in. *I'll be an elephant then, and what about you Henry?*

"I'll be an elephant too."

On another night we lay on the dock telling ghost stories (the girls inching their way closer to me until their heads were in my armpits); on another we played charades, but the best was when we made up scenes from favourite movies and acted them out. And every evening, Henry would leave just before the girls went to bed. And every night they would beg her to stay until one night she said, "Let's all go away together—to Kenya!"

The girls pleaded and jumped up and down and as she opened the door to leave she turned, looked at me and said, "I mean it, let's all of us go."

And I did think about it. I considered the possibility of getting up and leaving just like that. And I thought about that unspoken, unrevisited, unbelievable kiss. The girls pestered me of course, and I said that *maybe in the future, but not now*. And my eldest looked at me and said, "Dad would love it too!"

And then, just like that, the babies were gone, just as I knew they would be, I would later say. *Stupid bird* I said aloud, *didn't she realize the pine was broken, too small, no protection, an invitation to whatever or whoever was hungry.* No, the birds had not flown away I had to say, *they were too little, too small.* I softened and said *maybe*.

The girls were heartbroken as we lifted the nest out of the pine and placed it on our mantle. Have you ever held a nest—a small one, I mean? This nest looked fragile, but even now, years later after having been moved from mantle to kitchen counter to desk back to mantle, it has held its shape. So light, the little twigs woven together, knotted in fact. I wonder, as I imagine you have, whether or not another bird, another mother, might have reused it? That isn't the way things work, my girls remind me, every mother makes her own home.

Henry visited one last time before leaving for the city.

"I imagine we will run into each other at some point!" she said. Henry hugged each of the girls, and to say I didn't tremble slightly when she reached out her arms to me would be a lie.

Later when I was tidying up, I was drawn by an odd scent to my youngest daughter's bed where I found, under a pillow, a chapati. She said that she loved the smell, that it reminded her of Henry.

Just before leaving, I painted the final piece for the series. Catherine in Flight—Part Two. There out of the trees into the sky. The night before I left my eldest turned to me and said, "Did you tell anyone, well Henry, about my crush?"

I hadn't, and it wasn't a complete lie because you don't know his name.

"Good. I don't like him anymore."

We didn't see her again—Henry, that is. Not that summer, anyway. I did hear from her, though. She sent texts, maybe every few days. They always said the same thing: *miss you*. But I didn't answer. In October she came to my opening—her hair piled on her head, wearing a long purple-and-orange-striped dress that covered her wrists. Jeff was there, and the girls, thrilled to see Henry, introduced her to their dad.

"Ah, you gave her flight," she whispered.

I think of that kiss, of what might have happened had the girls not crushed open the door, their voices full of curiousity and excitement. I think of what might have happened had I asked Henry what she did during the day, I think of what might have happened had she ventured by in her kayak long before the dinner hour, when the sun still warmed the grass, when it was just me and my paints and a nest with budding life. I think what might have happened had we, I, taken her up on the offer of a Kenyan adventure. I think about what would have happened had I answered *me too*. But I didn't ask, she didn't venture by, and I didn't take her up on the offer. And then I think of that chapati and the small permanent stain now on the mattress cover and remind myself that I did the right thing.

A year later I will be in New York at the Met on a sketching course and I will look up and see her auburn hair piled up, just a few feet away from me. I will see her at a tennis match, on the adjoining side of a stadium and I will stare and lose track of the score. On a cold February night, I will be attending a poetry slam and she will get up and deliver, and I will pay attention only to her voice, remembering getting drunk on her stories. When the girls are teenagers we will be in Kenya, and I will see her thin, beautiful wrist wave as our mini-bus rolls by. I will stand and watch elephants at a watering hole, listen to insects at night, and by chance I'll find an empty nest, and I'll wonder.

THE FATHER KING
DOLLY REISMAN

CHARLIE STANDS OUTSIDE our old rusty green Saab with his nose pressed up to the backseat passenger side window.

"He's dead," he says. Charlie says it like he doesn't care. That or he is about to explode from keeping all that emotion inside him. I look for a tear or something visible. Maybe a slight tremor of his lip, the kind I have just thinking about my dog dying, even though my dog is alive and loving life. But there is nothing.

I nudge him over and plant my nose on the same window right beside him, so close that I can hear his nose hairs moving and some kind of whistling sound coming from his nasal passages, I swear.

"Fuck," I say, moving my head back, frantically erasing my breath before pressing my nose up against the window again to try and get another, better look. Mostly what I see are the car keys in the front seat passenger side where Charlie tossed them just before I hit the lock button.

"He looks the same as he looked last night when he was still breathing, Charlie," I say.

"You didn't even look at him."

That was the truth, but I wasn't going to let Charlie know that I had an aversion to dead people, especially when the dead person was our dad.

"And you can't tell from here if he's dead or not," I yell, as if louder means it has to be true.

"If we don't do something fast the heat is going to cook him. He'll be dead soon enough," Charlie says.

Dad is lying flat in the back seat splayed out like a slab of meat at a butcher shop. Charlie and I snuck him out of the hospital last night so we could take him on one last road trip before he died, because he was going to die, there was no doubt about that. One minute Dad was lying in the hospital bed with monitors crawling all over his thin, pale skin. He looked like he was about to levitate right up to heaven, when suddenly Charlie had him up and dressed in a pair of striped pajamas.

"Let's go," he said, grabbing a wheelchair and strapping Dad in like an infant so he didn't fall forward. I swore I saw a smile cross Dad's face just then, something that looked like happiness. This was one of the conversations Charlie and I kept having over the months Dad was in the hospital in what the doctors called a non-responsive state. Charlie was sure Dad was brain dead, where I saw the evidence of life in every twitch of his skin and flicker of his lashes.

"You're just seeing what you want to see," Charlie said. "Even the doctors said it was nothing more than an atavistic response."

I hated it when my Harvard-educated brother used big words. I'm sure he did it to make me feel bad for dropping out mid-semester of my final year of undergrad. Wasting our parents' precious savings when I did nothing with it. I dropped out the year our mother died in a fatal car crash. She was alone. Travelling on the DVP when the truck in front of her lost its load and smothered her in an avalanche of sand.

"Well it's better that than thinking he's just a corpse with a pulse," I said as we started the car and squealed out of the parking lot. Charlie drove getaway for the first hour or so, then I took over until my eyelids threatened closing.

I wipe the sweat off the back of my neck and look at my pink Mickey Mouse watch; the one Dad bought me when I turned five. The watch was an extra special gift from him for not showing up at my birthday party. It isn't even nine in the morning and the sun is blistering down on us. My whole body is moist and sticky.

"What the hell are we going to do?" I ask.

"Break the window."

"If we had something to break the window with, I would have done it by now. You think I'm stupid?"

Charlie gives me a death like glare. His right lip lifts just the tiniest bit like a snarling dog. "Don't make me answer that," he says.

Charlie blames me for my fast fingers on the locking device even though I try and explain to him I was attempting to unlock the door, but my sweaty hands slipped. "I knew we shouldn't have taken him out of the hospital," I say.

"He was dying," Charlie says.

"That was the reason not to take him out. So he didn't die here in the middle of bloody nowhere." I pull my sleeve across my face to sop up the sudden gush of tears.

"We could just leave him here, you know. The car could be his coffin," Charlie says.

I check out the area. It's about an hour's drive from Vegas. We had planned on a Death Valley expedition, but we are having a desert death instead, somewhere on a dusty road where no one else travels.

"We could all die here if we don't get inside the car and get going. Did you go off trail?" I ask.

One more please-drop-dead stare from Charlie. He runs his hand through his hair, catching his thin wedding ring on one of his springy curls.

I shrug. "Well, it was dark, it's possible you took a wrong turn."

Charlie gives me the finger. "You were driving the last bit."

Stifling a laugh, I gulp and swallow air. My saliva is thick and pasty. Christ, I hate the feeling of cotton in my mouth.

"Where's the water?" I say.

Charlie points to the car. "Locked inside with Pops."

"Fuck me dead," I say. Then I start banging on the windows, trying to punch them out. Charlie takes off his shirt, rolls it up, and hands it to me.

"Wrap your knuckles with this. We don't need you bleeding to death out here and dying too."

"Whaaahhh," I scream as I run at the car and punch the window like I was used to cutting glass with my hands. "We need a rock. Or a piece of steel or something."

Just beyond us is nothing but flat sunbaked desert. The kind you die in. That's when I start crying again.

Charlie comes over and stands with his hands awkwardly at his side, not knowing what to do. Big gobs of snot slide out my nose and down my face. I can feel every bit of moisture leaking out my cracks—god, I wish my skin wasn't so lined— and I know I should stop but I start howling even more.

We had stopped for the night because both of us were too tried to drive one more bit. The moon was new and the stars carpeted the entire sky.

"Dad, they're twinkling for us," I said.

I turned and looked into the back seat where Dad was stretched out in the exact position we had put him in when we escaped the hospital. His eyes were open, and I assumed he was looking at the stars that seemed to shimmer with a *welcome home* message. I didn't know how much of Dad was really there, if his brain was functioning properly after all the damage from the stroke, but without all the coils and machines cluttering his face and the now halo glow of stars, he looked almost normal. He was alive.

"Dad, can you see the Big Dipper there?"

I was sure he followed my finger to where it was pointing, but he didn't utter a sound, not even an appreciative grunt. In the hospital they had performed a pencil test, watching as his eyes followed it or not. Unresponsive. We didn't ask them exactly what that meant, it just sounded dire.

"I think he understands," I said.

"Doubt it," Charlie said.

I was too tired to argue. It was enough to be in the same car looking at the same sky, the three of us sharing the air and breathing in each other's thoughts and dreams. Dad was calm; he was comforted. There wasn't a hint of anguish, and I knew then that Charlie had made the right decision in bringing him to the desert so he could die untethered with a sense of the open sky and endless possibilities.

"Think he'll see mom up there?" I asked.

Charlie didn't answer for a minute or two then he squeaked out, *I sure hope so*, and nothing else.

Morning comes with a welcome blast of heat and sun. I check to make sure Dad is still with us. I watch his thin rib cage rise and fall like I do my infant daughter's chest when she's sleeping on her back, her pure soul self-trusting of the entire world. Dad's in that state now, a return to childhood, to the beginning of time. I wonder if his soul is lined up to be placed inside that of a soon-to-be-born baby. The thought excites and saddens me at the same time. If he does become someone else, he won't see our mom. My thoughts on reincarnation are thin and unformed, but I do wonder right then: *What if all of this is preordained, even us being locked out of the car?*

"Come on Charlie," I say. "Let's ram the window open. We gotta do something."

Charlie grabs my arms and wraps mine around his waist and then his arms around me. We charge the car window and run as hard as we can, smashing into the glass. It's hard and resilient, but I can feel the tiniest give and see the smallest crack.

"One more time," Charlie says, grabbing me again as we scream at the bloody window to break open. And it does.

I check my dad's pulse. It's faint, but it's there. Charlie grabs the water bottle and puts it up to my father's mouth. He takes a few sips and then like some miracle he opens his eyes, looks at the two of us, his progeny. It's a look I recognize, the look of the old and of the newborn. The look of life and the look of death. He nods to us, almost imperceptibly.

"Time to get going," Charlie says.

We are at the hospital. The doctors tell us of new innovations for people with strokes. We suck on watermelon and let the fruit dissolve on Dad's lips as the juices drip all over his face, spreading into his mouth and all down his body like a watermelon bath. Sticky and gooey and sweet, a covering for a father king. All I want is a sign of what to do when a blaze of sun angles across the room, a perfect beam showing us the way home.

Rea Tarvydas lives and writes in Calgary, Alberta, Canada. Her work can be found in *The New Quarterly, The Fiddlehead, Grain*, and *Writing Menopause: An Anthology of Fiction, Poetry and Creative Non-fiction* (Inanna, 2017). She is the winner of the 2012 Brenda Strathern "Late Bloomers" Writing Prize and has been nominated for a National Magazine Award. Her debut book of short stories, *How To Pick Up a Maid in Statue Square*, was published by Thistledown Press (2016) and shortlisted for the ReLit Prize (2017). Please visit her website: www.reatarvydas.com.

Anna Rumin began writing stories during quiet time when she was banished to her bedroom for an hour every afternoon. She began married life in the Eastern Townships of Quebec, where she joined the faculty at the Bishop's University School of Education and where her children were born. Her graduate work was rooted in narrative inquiry and the role life-stories play in education. After ten years in Quebec, her family packed up and moved to Switzerland, where she continued to teach, write, and travel at almost every opportunity. Now in Ottawa, Anna writes short fiction, designs and teaches memoir-based writing courses, spends precious time at her cottage with friends and family, and continues to consume good fiction.

Dolly Reisman is a writer and sometimes producer. Her short story "Driving 1-95" was published on Jewishfiction. net, issue #18. Other short fiction has been published in the *Maple Tree Literary Supplement* and her short story "Doba" was anthologized in *TOK: Writing the New Toronto—Book 2*. Her haiku "Found Youth" won second prize in Diaspora Dialogues' LitToronto Map contest. *A Different Man*, her play about Albert Speer, was produced in 2008 in New Zealand. Dolly is working on a collection of connected short stories tentatively called, *Oy, That Nietzsche*. She lives in Toronto.

Sarah Selecky Writing School x Invisible Publishing:
Pocket books that celebrate phenomenal writing

The Little Bird Writing Contest is an international contest for innovative, emerging short fiction writers. The contest opens each spring when the birds come back and showcases the excellent stories that come from **Sarah Selecky Writing School**'s daily writing prompts. Each winning story is chosen by a celebrated author and published in a beautiful anthology. Proceeds from anthology sales go towards the Pelee Island Bird Observatory and the Prince Edward Point Bird Observatory to help protect the real little birds out there.

Invisible Publishing produces cool and contemporary Canadian fiction, creative non-fiction, and poetry. As a not-for-profit publisher, we are committed to publishing diverse voices and stories in beautifully designed and affordable editions. Even though we're small in scale, we take our work and our mission seriously: we believe in building communities that sustain and encourage engaging, literary, and current writing.

For more information visit invisiblepublishing.com and sarahseleckywritingschool.com

Sarah Selecky
WRITING SCHOOL